Words to Know Before You Read

activities

argue

directions

fountain

imagination

ingredients

picnic

recipe

www.rourkepublishing.com

Edited by Luana Mitten
Illustrated by Ed Meyer
Art Direction and Page Layout by Renee Brady

Library of Congress Cataloging-in-Publication Data

Moreta, Gladys
Too Much TV / Gladys Moreta.
p. cm. -- (Little Birdie Books)
ISBN 978-1-61741-815-0 (hard cover) (alk. paper)
ISBN 978-1-61236-019-5 (soft cover)
Library of Congress Control Number: 2011924666

Rourke Publishing
Printed in the United States of America, North Mankato, Minnesota
060711
060711CL

www.rourkepublishing.com - rourke@rourkepublishing.com
Post Office Box 643328 Vero Beach, Florida 32964

Too Much TV!

Written by Gladys Moreta
Illustrated by Ed Meyer

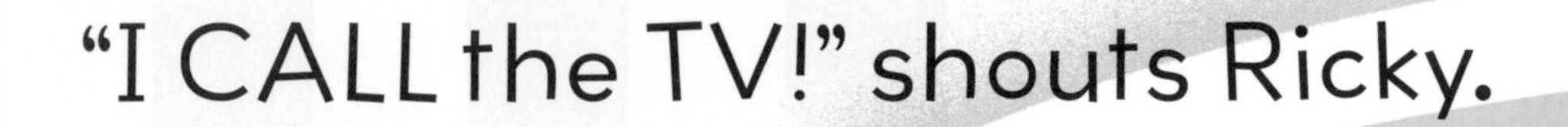

"I CALL the TV!" shouts Ricky.

"No, I'm watching my show!" cries Ava.

"My show is starting!" snarls Ricky.

"No, I get to choose!" screams Ava.

"They're watching too much TV. Every day they argue over the TV," complains Mom.

“Let’s talk to them. Kids come here,” calls Dad.

“I’m watching TV!” shouts Ricky.

“I want to watch TV!” cries Ava.

"Ricky, give me the control!" demands Ava.

"No!" snaps Ricky.

Mom shouts, "EVERYBODY FREEZE!"

"You're watching too much TV," says Mom.

"But what else can we do?" asked Ricky.

“Think about it. Use your imagination,” says Mom sternly.

"This is boring," says Ava. "What can we do now?"

"I'm hungry," states Ricky. "Let's make sandwiches and have a picnic."

"Remember when we made a Mentos Diet Coke Fountain with Grandma?" asks Ava.

"Yeah!" says Ricky.

"Mom, can we make a Mentos Diet Coke fountain?"

"Sure Ava, get the recipe box," Mom says.

Mom suggested that I look for the directions under the letter M.

"We need more Diet Coke and some mint Mentos," says Ava.

"Dad," says Ricky. "We need some ingredients for our Mentos fountain."

“What do you need?” says Dad. “I’ll go to the store.”

“Let’s read some books until Dad gets back,” suggests Mom.

"Dad is home. Let's make the fountain!" yells Ava.

How to Make a Mentos Diet Coke Fountain

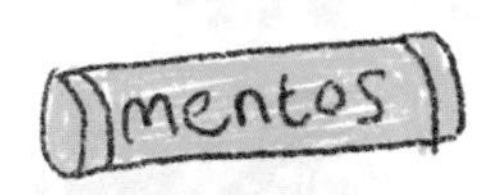

Things You Will Need:

One pack of mint Mentos

One liter bottle of Diet Coke

1. Take the bottle of Diet Coke and the pack of Mentos outside.

2. Drop 3 or 4 Mentos into the bottle of Diet Coke. (For a bigger splash, put the whole pack of Mentos into the bottle of Diet Coke.)

3. Stand back, or you'll be taking a Diet Coke shower.

diet
COKE
mentos

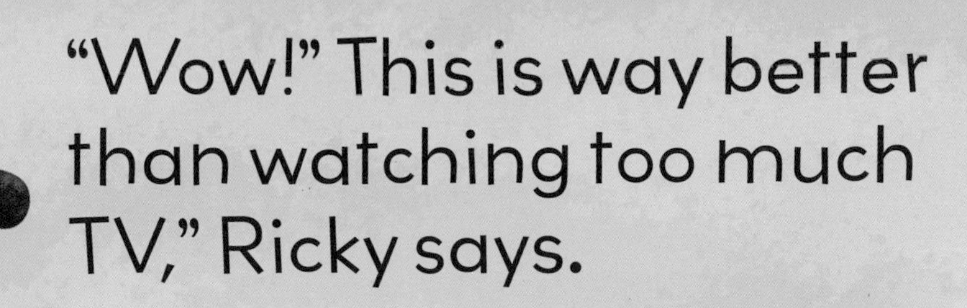

"Wow!" This is way better than watching too much TV," Ricky says.

Fun Things to Do Besides Watching TV

1. Make a Mentos Diet Coke Fountain.
2. Have a picnic.
3. Play board games.
4. Read books.
5. Cook dinner with Mom.
6. Spend time with Grandma.

After Reading Activities

You and the Story...

Why did Mom and Dad decide Ricky and Ava were watching too much TV?

What happened when Mom said they couldn't watch any more TV?

Do you ever watch too much TV? If so, what are some other things you could do besides watching TV?

Words You Know Now...

The words below are missing letters. Write each word on a piece of paper and fill-in the missing letters.

__tivities

__gue

__rections

fount___

__agination

__gredients

pichn__

__cipe

You Could...Try Your Own Experiments at Home

- Make a list of experiments or activities you would like to try at home.
- Now choose just one experiment to complete.
- Make a list of the materials you will need to complete your activity.
- Decide where and when you will complete your activity.
- Write the instructions for completing your activity.

Remember...Safety First!

Always ask an adult for help before you start an experiment.

About the Author

Gladys Moreta lives in Kissimmee, Florida with her husband and their two wonderful boys. Her boys and husband love watching TV but they also like doing fun activities together as a family.

About the Illustrator

Ed Myer is a Manchester-born illustrator now living in London. After growing up in an artistic household, Ed studied ceramics at university but always continued drawing pictures. As well as illustration, Ed likes traveling , playing computer games and walking little Ted (his Jack russell).